We love our dogs.
They bring us unconditional love and happiness
and they never complain
(partly because they can't speak).

Dogs live in the 'now'...no regrets, no worries.
If we humans could live like dogs
the world would be a far happier place.

This book is dedicated to all the great dogs
who've lived a full and happy life.

Especially Carlos our cocker spaniel

First published in Great Britain in 2022

All cartoons copyright Neil Kerber 2022

copyright Neil Kerber 2022.

For Lilia and Tilly xxx

And huge thanks to
Carlos our cocker spaniel
for all your help and advice
in putting this book together.

Kesler

"HAS ANYONE EVER TOLD YOU YOU'VE GOT THE MOST BEAUTIFUL EYE GUNK ?!"

(Published in
Private Eye
magazine)

TODAY I'M GOING
TO HOLD IN
ALL MY FARTS
THEN LET OUT
ONE HUGE STINKER
WHILE THEY'RE
HAVING DINNER

10 IMPORTANT FACTS ABOUT DOGS:

1. Dogs are always happy
2. Dogs are always happy
3. Dogs are always happy
4. Dogs are always happy
5. Dogs are always happy
6. Dogs are always happy
7. Dogs are always happy
8. Dogs are always happy
9. Dogs eat poo
10. Dogs are always happy

My parents are coming over...
get the **nice** dog out...
put this one away!!!

okay honey!

DING DONG!

DOG BREEDS THAT
NEVER SURVIVED:
no: 86319
"DILLMATION"

Half dalmation,
half dill pickle

"FAKEDOGCOMPLIMENTPHOBIA"

The fear of having to say
someone's dog is cute
when they're clearly not

Be honest with me honey, d'you think I'm moulting on top?

DOGS of CULTURE

Let's go to the art gallery. There's an exhibition of Pre-Raphaelite paintings that we can wee on!

FLEAS:

DogWalk Rage

DOGGY PHOTOS:

first time
in the park

first time
off lead

first time he runs off
without you noticing
because you're too busy
sharing doggy pics
on social media

I just find that if I cock my leg up I can't get all the dribbles out!

CATS

One of the more annoying characteristics of cats is their tendancy to appear in the middle of a dog book, without any reason, other than to annoy all the dogs.

AWKWARD DOG MINGLING

the anatomy of a dog

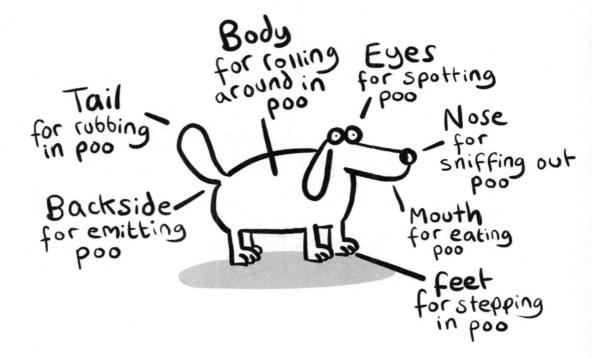

Tail for rubbing in poo

Body for rolling around in poo

Eyes for spotting poo

Nose for sniffing out poo

Backside for emitting poo

Mouth for eating poo

feet for stepping in poo

Sir I'd like to ask permission for your daughter's butt to sniff!

DOG TATTOOS

AAAAH SWEET...
THEIR TAILS
ARE WAGGING,
SO THEY MUST
BE PLAYING!
YOU #@!!!
...YOU SLEPT
WITH MY
WIFE...
I'M GONNA
KILL YOU!!!
GRRRRR.....
Kesler

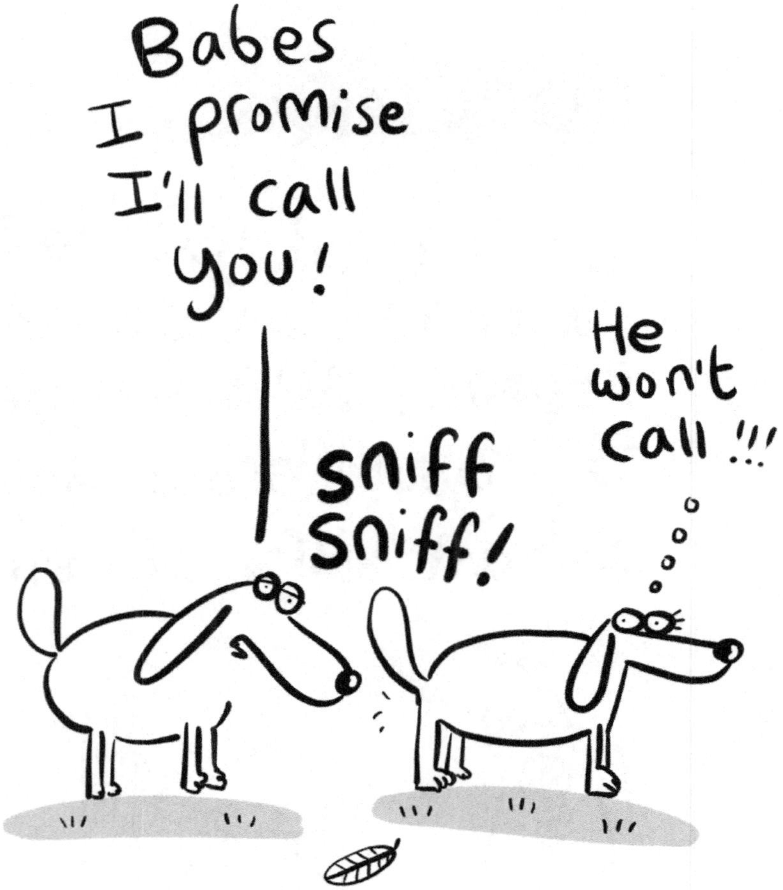
Babes I promise I'll call you!
sniff sniff!
He won't call !!!

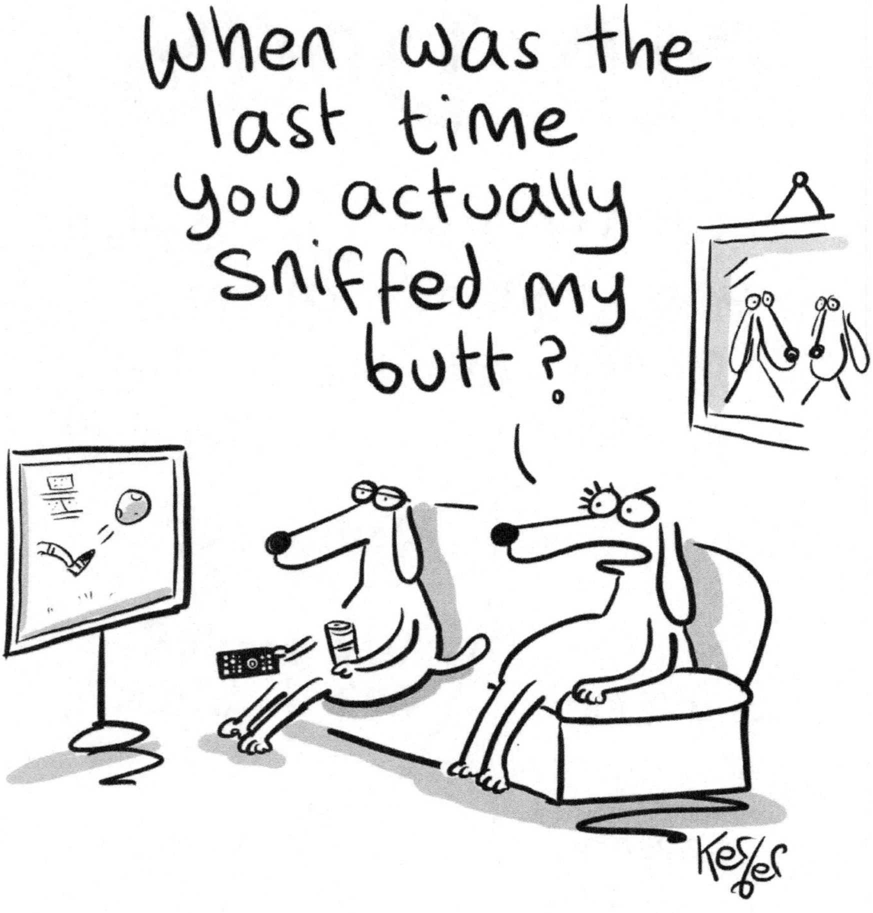
When was the last time you actually sniffed my butt?

Why you never see dog tennis umpires...

OMG — tennis ball !!!

Kesler

SCENE FROM GANGSTER MOVIE
DOGFELLAS:

"AND OVER THERE, ACROSS THE ROOM, STOOD JIMMY TWO SNIFFS, SO-CALLED BECAUSE HE ALWAYS SNIFFED A BUTT TWICE" ...

I'M GONNA GO SNIFF A BUTT SNIFF A BUTT!

Kesler

OLD DOG FOOD ADVERT ACTORS REMINISCE:

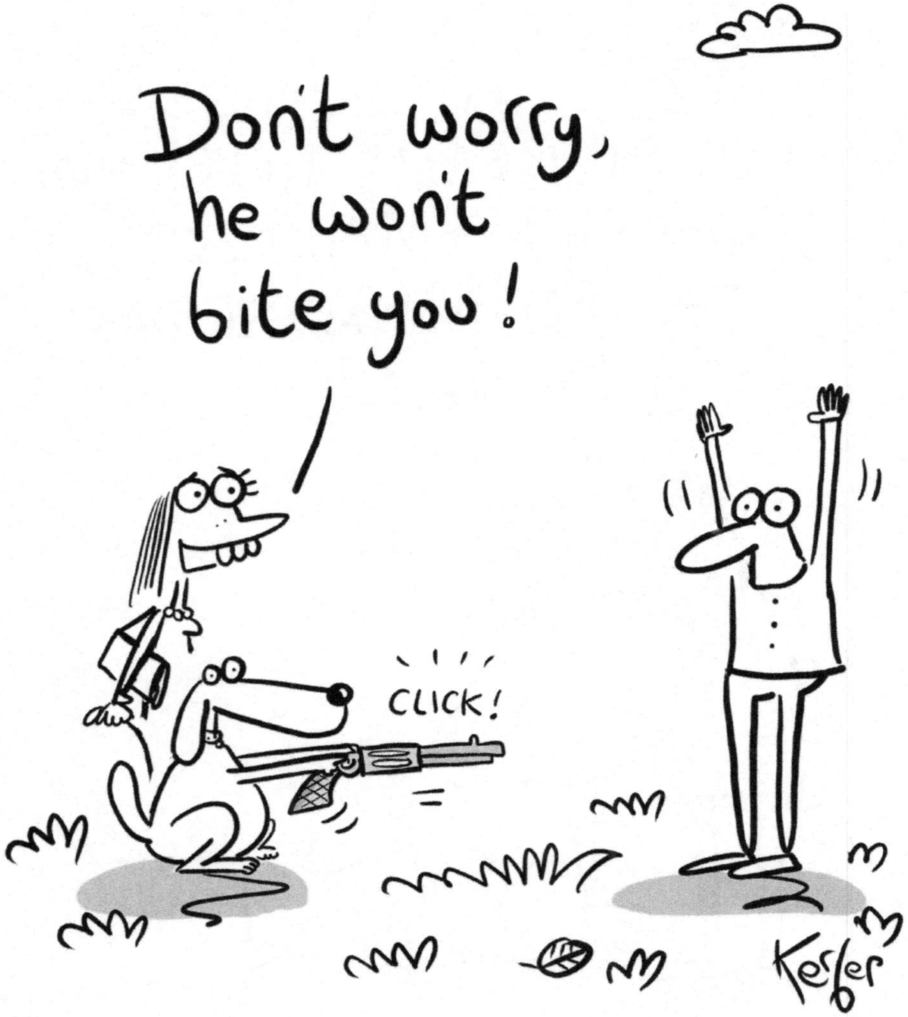
Don't worry, he won't bite you!
CLICK!
Kerler

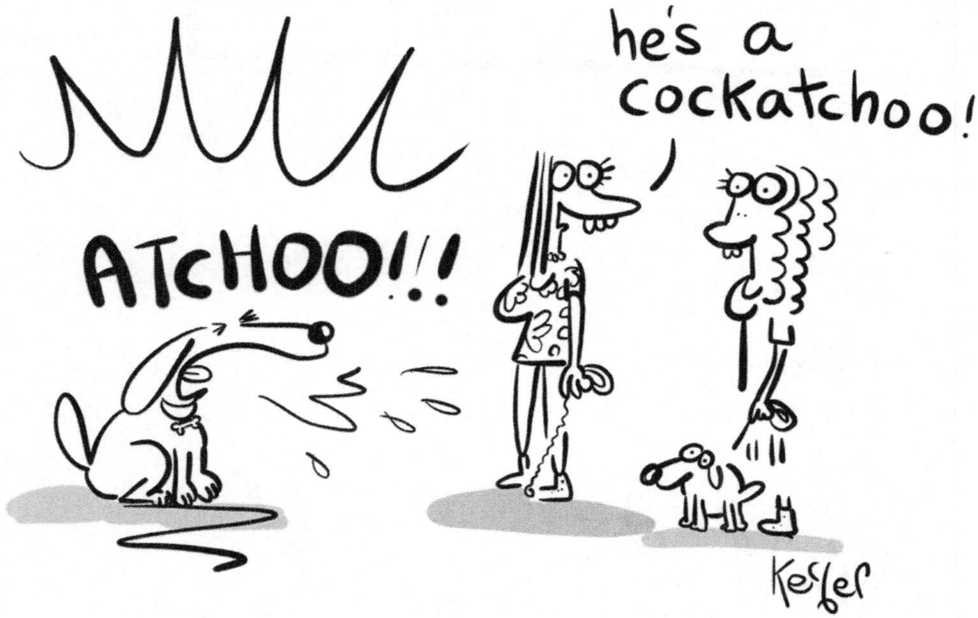
ATCHOO!!!
he's a cockatchoo!
Kerber

is it a bitch?
yeah I'M in the fashion industry dahling! I hate you!!!
Grrrr...
Kerber

for the Dog who
doesn't have to try
too hard

DOG OWNER CHIT-CHAT...

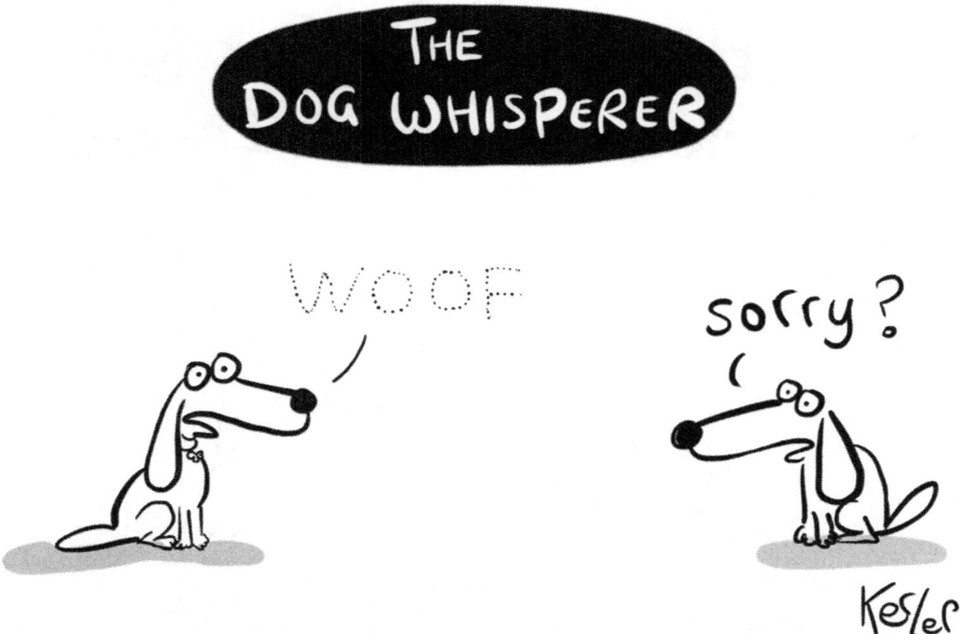
THE DOG WHISPERER
WOOF
sorry?
Kester

"...And from that moment on, the dog and the bee became best friends"

(Basically, we can't think of a decent punchline for this cartoon)

Finally, a huge Thank You
to all the doggies
who've appeared in this book...

Printed in Great Britain
by Amazon